HOLLY KELLER

GERALDINE'S BIG SNOW

Greenwillow Books  New York

TO HELIOS,

FOR

WARMTH

AND

INSPIRATION

Watercolors were used for
the full-color illustrations.
The text type is Times Roman.

Library of Congress Cataloging-in-Publication Data

Keller, Holly.   Geraldine's big snow.
Summary: Geraldine can't wait for the snow to come
so that she can coast down the hill on her sled.
[1. Snow—Fiction]   I. Title.   PZ7.K28132Sn   1988
[E]   87-14936   ISBN 0-688-07513-4
ISBN 0-688-07514-2 (lib. bdg.)

Geraldine brought her new sled down from the attic and put her boots near the door. "I'm ready," she said.

"It will come faster if you don't watch
so much," Mama told her.
But Geraldine wanted to watch.

"Tell me again what Papa heard on the radio,"
  she said.
"This is the last time, Geraldine," Mama scolded.
"He heard that there is a big storm coming,
  and there will be at least a foot of snow."

"How much is a foot?" Geraldine asked.
  Mama held out her hand.
"Wow," Geraldine said, sucking in her cheeks.
"But when?"
"Soon," said Mama. "Very soon."

Geraldine put on her hat and her jacket.
"I'm going outside to wait."
"Good," Mama said.

"Hello, Geraldine," said Mrs. Wilson, who
was coming home from the market.
"You bought a lot of apples," Geraldine said.
Mrs. Wilson nodded. "It will be hard to go
shopping when the snow comes."

Geraldine walked along with her eyes on the sky until she bumped into Mr. Peters, who was coming home from the library.

"'Afternoon, Geraldine," Mr. Peters grumbled
as he picked up his books.
"I'm sorry," Geraldine said. "I was watching
for the snow."
Mr. Peters cleared his throat. "Better get plenty
of good books to read."

Geraldine stopped to watch Mr. Harper
put seeds in his bird feeder.
"Birds get hungry in the snow," he said.

Uncle Albert was attaching the snowplow to his truck. He waved to Geraldine, and Geraldine waved back.

Geraldine started to sing. "It's coming,
it's coming, it's coming." She sang all the
way home and watched the sky.

But by suppertime there was still no snow,
and Geraldine was weary from watching.

"Maybe it isn't really coming," she said.
"Maybe the man on the radio is wrong.
   Maybe Mrs. Wilson, and Mr. Peters, and
   Mr. Harper, and Uncle Albert are all wrong."

Geraldine took a last look out the window.

A star was hiding behind a cloud, and
she watched it until she fell asleep.

Then in the night it came.
Softly and quietly.
Millions of snowflakes piled up
on houses and trees.
They made soft mounds on
the streets and in the park, and
beautiful crystals on the windows.

Geraldine heard Uncle Albert's
snowplow before she opened
her eyes.
"It's here!" she shouted. "It's here!"

Mrs. Wilson got right to work
making apple pies.

Mr. Peters sat in front of the fireplace reading.

Mr. Harper counted eleven finches
and three cardinals at his bird feeder.

And Geraldine took her sled to the top
of the highest hill in the park—

and coasted all the way down.